PART ONE

Finding

the

Hat

We found a hat.

We found it together.

But there is only one hat.

And there are two of us.

How does it look on me?

It looks good on you.

How does it look on me?

It looks good on you too.

It looks good on both of us.

But it would not be right
if one of us had a hat
and the other did not.

There is only one thing to do.
We must leave the hat here
and forget that we found it.

PART TWO

Watching

the

Sunset

We are watching the sunset.

We are watching it together.

What are you thinking about?

I am thinking about the sunset.

What are you thinking about?

Nothing.

PART THREE

Going

to

Sleep

We are going to sleep.

We are going to sleep here together.

Are you almost asleep?

I am almost asleep.

Are you all the way asleep?

I am all the way asleep.
I am dreaming a dream.

What are you dreaming about?

I will tell you what I am dreaming about.

I am dreaming that
I have a hat.
It looks very good
on me.

You are also there.
You also have a hat.

It looks very good on you too.

We both have hats?